BRANISLAV
THE
DRAGON
A new tale of old Russia

By Mary Lou Masey

Illustrated by Helen Basilevsky

DAVID McKAY CO

BRANISLAV THE DRAGON

BRANISLAV THE DRAGON

ONCE upon a time, long, long ago, there was a dragon named Branislav. Branislav, whose father was King of the Dragons, lived deep in the land of Russia, in a castle.

Now everyone knows that dragons are fierce and ill-tempered. But Branislav was different. The only time he breathed fire was to warm himself. He did not care to frighten people, or capture fair maidens, or fight knights — any of the things that dragons are supposed to do. What he really liked was to lie around the castle, wagging his tail, and watching the comings and goings of the castle servants.

His favorite place was the kitchen, with its great roaring fireplace and its huge platters of meat pies and steaming cauldrons of soup. But just before dawn, he would trail after the old peasant women and help them gather mushrooms. Everyone got so used to Branislav around the castle that no one ever paid any attention to him.

One morning Branislav's father, who was the fiercest dragon of all, was coming back to the castle after an expedition. Whom should he spy in the woods but Branislav, happily picking mushrooms.

"Bozhe moi!" roared his father. "My son, a dragon, gathering mushrooms like an old woman!" He stomped up to Branislav and shouted, "Why aren't you off with your brothers fighting knights? Don't let me set eyes on you until you've captured at least one maiden!"

So Branislav crept glumly down to the
river and unhitched one of his father's
rowboats. He rowed and rowed. Big

tears rolled down his cheeks and splashed
into the bottom of the boat. Every so
often, he would have to stop and bail
it out.

One morning as the sun rose, Brani-slav saw in the distance the glittering turrets of a little Russian village zamok, or castle. "If I know Russian villages," he said to himself, "there will be an old prince in that zamok, with a daughter named Olga." So he tied his rowboat to a tree and waited for nightfall.

As soon as it was dark Branislav got up his courage and set forth for the village. Tippy tippy toe he went, through the narrow winding streets, until he reached the zamok.

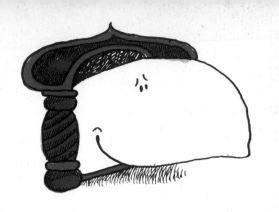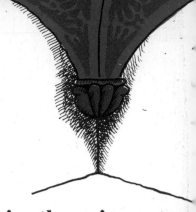

Branislav stuck his nose in the window of the zamok and sure enough, there was the princess Olga, bored as anything, lying on her bed, looking at the ceiling. With a polite cough, Branislav introduced himself. "My name is Branislav," he said.

The princess turned over to look at him and raised one eyebrow. "I suppose you mean to drag me off," she said. "Just wait until I pack my things." She leaped up and began to pile her dresses into a suitcase. Then she dragged the suitcase through the window onto Branislav's back and climbed atop.

When the prince discovered next morning that his daughter was gone, he let it be known throughout the land that the lucky bogatyr, or knight, who found his daughter would have her hand in marriage as well as a goodly portion of his kingdom.

Of all the bogatyrs who came to the castle, three were chosen. The first was called Vanya. Vanya had a beautiful black mustache, and his armor was so shiny that nobody could look at it without squinting.

Next was Ilya. He had no armor but he had invented a dragon-catching machine which he was very anxious to try.

The third bogatyr was named Alyosha.
Alyosha had no armor and no dragon-
catching machine, but he was so brave
and strong and handsome that it didn't
matter.

All three bogatyrs shook hands,
climbed on their horses and set off into
the forest.

Meanwhile Olga and Branislav, all unaware, had drifted across the river and had tied up their boat to a tree. They were happily lunching on mushrooms when suddenly Olga saw the three bogatyrs.

"My father has done it again!" she cried. "I can never get farther than the other side of the river. Branislav, you will have to fight them. I am not going back to that boring castle."

Vanya was the first to reach the river. He stuck his toe in the water and jumped. "I don't mind fighting a dragon," he muttered, "but I don't feel like getting soaked." He wiped the splashes off his armor and went home.

Next Ilya scrambled down to the edge of the water, lugging his raft on which sat the dragon-catching machine. But his foot slipped, and all fell in — Ilya, the raft and the dragon machine. While Ilya was rising up, up, up, to the top, the dragon machine was sinking down, down, down to the bottom. There was nothing to do but go home, too. Poor Ilya!

But Alyosha dove right into the river and swam and swam until he reached the other side. He wasn't even out of breath when he climbed up on the bank. Olga's heart went pitter patter. She had never seen anyone so handsome.

Meanwhile Branislav had taken refuge behind a pine tree and was shivering and shaking with fright. It was bad enough having your lunch interrupted without having to fight a whole bunch of strangers.

Olga ran to the boat and grabbed her suitcase. "Help, help!" she cried. "Please rescue me from this wicked dragon."

"Never fear," said Alyosha stoutly. "I have come especially to rescue you. But hark! What is that sound of sniffling behind that tree?"

"It's Branislav," answered Olga. She began to feel rather sad. "He isn't really wicked. We are quite good friends, in fact. Oh, I can't bear the thought of leaving him behind! Branislav, please come out."

But Branislav, who had been peeking around the corner, ducked back again behind the tree.

"Oh dear, his feelings are hurt. What shall we do?" asked Olga.

"Don't worry!" cried Alyosha. "I have an idea! We can get him a job in your father's kitchen. Branislav's fire breather will really come in handy for roasting, and lighting the castle fireplaces and things."

At this, Branislav came timidly out from his hiding place, wagging his tail with joy.

So off they went all three down the river. On the third day they turned a bend and there at the pier were Olga's father, the prince, and all the bogatyrs and peasants of the kingdom, cheering and waving banners. There was even a red carpet rolled down for Olga and Alyosha to walk on to the zamok.

Olga's father, the prince, smothered Alyosha in a furry embrace. "Everyone for miles around has heard of your triumph!" he cried. "The birds of the air and the animals of the fields have kept us informed of your progress. Now you shall have your reward. We shall have a marvelous wedding feast, the like of which has never been seen in all the Russias! Ask of me any favor you wish and I shall grant it."

"Thank you, sire," said Alyosha. "I do have a favor to ask. Would you give Branislav a job in the kitchen? And please don't be angry at him for kidnaping Olga. He didn't mean it."

"Very well," cried the prince, "although it seems to me very strange that a dragon should desire such a position. However, as he did my daughter no harm, I cannot bear him any great ill will. So be it, dragon!"

As dawn rose on the morning of the wedding feast, there sat Branislav by the fireplace in the kitchen, trying to start up his fire breather. Piles and piles of meat waited to be roasted and skewers of shashlik to be flambéd, and all the fireplaces — two hundred and seventy-nine, to be exact — to be lighted. Branislav huffed and he puffed but all he could raise up was big rusty clouds of smoke.

"It is out of order from not being used," cried the head chef impatiently. "You are smoking up the whole castle, Branislav."

At last a few sparks came and then, to wild acclaim, a beautiful blaze of flames. Then there were such hurryings and scurryings, and bubblings and boilings, and flourings and scourings, and roastings and toastings, the likes of which had never been seen before.

And indeed it was the most marvelous feast ever to be held in all the Russias, before or since.

And Alyosha and Olga lived happily ever after, with Branislav to keep the home fires burning.

THE  END